PUZZLE HEROES

ANCIENT ROME

ANNA NILSEN

ILLUSTRATED BY
DAVID LOPEZ

W
FRANKLIN WATTS
LONDON · SYDNEY

CONTENTS

5 - 7   THE QUEST BEGINS

8 - 9   THE CITY OF ROME

10 - 11   ROMAN MOSAICS

12 - 13   ROMAN BATHS

14 - 15   ROMAN THEATRE

16 - 17   THE CHARIOT RACE

18 - 19   THE ROMAN EMPERORS' GALLERY

20 - 21   INSPECTING ROMAN SOLDIERS

22 - 23   THE BATTLE OF ZAMA

24 - 25   CAESAR MEETS CLEOPATRA

26 - 27   THE EMPEROR'S BANQUET

28-30   ANSWERS

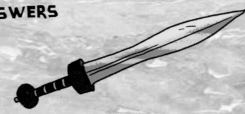

THE QUEST BEGINS

THE MAP OF THE ROMAN EMPIRE

NW · N · NE
W · E
SW · S · SE

BRITAIN

FRANCE

SPAIN

NORTH AFRICA

ROME

GREECE

TURKEY

MEDITERRANEAN SEA

ISRAEL

EGYPT

I'll be your guide to the puzzles you encounter on your journey.

THE CHARACTERS

GRANNY   LEAH   ZAK   GRANDAD

Meet Zak and Leah. They, and their family, are time - and space - travellers.

The children are learning about ancient Rome at school. Granny thinks that they will learn a lot about Roman history if they visit ancient Rome. Grandad wants to come too. So, one day, they all gather their gear and head into the past!

GRANNY DISAPPEARS!

The children are amazed by the Romans and gather lots of information for their school project. Then, one day, Granny disappears! Grandad receives a letter from a powerful Roman senator. 'If you want your wife to get home alive, you must solve all my puzzles!'

ARE YOU A PUZZLE HERO?

Granny needs all the help she can get! Can you help Zak, Leah and Grandad solve all the puzzles and get Granny released? There are lots of Roman gods to find and places to visit and get lost in if you aren't careful!

THE PUZZLES

SOLVE THE CRIME

Grandad has discovered a time-travel competition to crack an unsolved old Roman crime on the Internet. Can you be the first to solve it?

Treasure has been stolen by a gang of ten thieves. To find the treasure, collect the letters scattered around each scene. Work out the anagram to find where the treasure is hidden in that scene. What are the ten treasures? A different thief from the gang is hidden in each scene as well. They are all wearing the same type of toga. Can you find the ten thieves?

ROMAN GODS DOMINOES

The ancient Romans believed in lots of gods and goddesses who controlled all aspects of nature and daily life. This puzzle follows a chain of dominoes with pictures of Roman gods. Search each spread to find the domino that continues the 'chain' below:

The next domino could be anywhere in the book. You'll know when you've found the final one because there's no domino to continue the chain. How many dominoes are in the chain? Which god is on the final picture?

EAGLE BROOCHES AND THE KNOT OF HERCULES

Eagles were the symbol of the Roman army.

Hercules was a god known for his strength and courage. The knot of Hercules is a strong knot made by two intertwined ropes. It was known in ancient Rome as a protective amulet and a wedding symbol.

There are lots of brooches and knots to find in every scene. You must count and check you have spotted them all.

MORE TO FIND!

On every spread, you will also be challenged to find:

 Some weapons.

 A Roman animal coin.

 Items the Roman gods have lost in 'Meet the gods'.

 Grandad's carving passion — what has he made now?

THE CHAMELEON HUNT

Zak and Leah brought their pet chameleon with them from an earlier adventure in Egypt. It has escaped again! Can you help Zak and Leah find it on each spread?

ROMAN NUMERALS

You will need the table below to help you work out the Roman Emperors puzzle on pages 18-19.

Roman numerals use seven letters from the alphabet. The table below shows you the value for each of these numerals. Roman numerals are put together in a specific order to represent numbers.

Numerals (their values) are added together when written in groups, so XX = 20 (because 10+10 = 20). However, you cannot put more than three of the same numerals together. So you can write III for three, but you can't use IIII. Instead, four is shown with IV. If a letter with a smaller value is placed before a letter with a larger value, you subtract the smaller from the larger.

1 = I	14 = XIV
2 = II	15 = XV
3 = III	16 = XVI
4 = IV	17 = XVII
5 = V	18 = XVIII
6 = VI	19 = XIX
7 = VII	20 = XX
8 = VIII	30 = XXX
9 = IX	40 = XL
10 = X	50 = L
11 = XI	100 = C
12 = XII	500 = D
13 = XIII	1,000 = M

Some examples:

LIV = 54: L (50) + IV (4)

XXXIX = 39: XXX (10+10+10), IX (9)

CCXXXVII = 237: CC (100+100), XXX (10+10+10) and VII (5+2).

ROMAN EMPERORS

The emperors were the men who ruled over the Roman empire. The first emperor ruled Rome after years of fighting between rival leaders. Here is a chart of the reigns of some notable Roman emperors.

AUGUSTUS 27 BCE-14 CE	HADRIAN 117-138 CE
TIBERIUS 14-37 CE	MARCUS AURELIUS 161-180 CE
CALIGULA 37-41 CE	ELAGABALUS 218-222 CE
CLAUDIUS 41-54 CE	MAXIMINUS I 235-238 CE
NERO 54-68 CE	CONSTANTINE THE GREAT 306-337 CE
TITUS 79-81 CE	FLAVIUS VALENS 364-378 CE
TRAJAN 98-117 CE	JUSTINIAN I 527-565 CE

MATHS HELPER

If you get stuck with the puzzle on pages 12-13, this will help.

First count the swimmers. Count the number of women and divide the number by two. Then count the number of children and divide the number by four. Add on the number of men you counted and make a note of this number. Now divide the £60 by this number and it will give you the entry price for men, halve it to get the price for women, halve it again to get the price for children. (To check, if you multiply each price by the number of men, women and children you should reach the total of the income taken.) Repeat for the non-swimmers (but divide the £8.40).

THE CITY OF ROME

The centre of the Roman Empire was the city of Rome in what is now Italy. Rome was the greatest city of its time. At one time it had nearly one million people living there. The Romans were great builders and Rome was packed with great buildings including the Colosseum – the large stadium where the Romans watched gladiator fights.

THE COLOSSEUM

 Wild lions have escaped from the Colosseum! Your task is to catch the lions and get them back to their cages in the Colosseum. Start at the green flag to the south of the city. You must find the route with the most lions on it finishing at the Colosseum (pink flag).

You must not turn back or go over the same route twice. Watch you don't get bitten. Always approach the lions from behind.

MEET THE GODS
 Mercury was the Roman god of finance, gymnasts, thieves, merchants and commerce and the messenger of the gods. He had winged sandals, a winged hat and carried a magic wand. Can you find them?

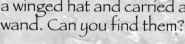

COIN
As well as being used as military animals, elephants also appeared as entertainment at the Colosseum. Can you find the elephant coin?

LOST WEAPONS
 How many of each of these weapons can you find?

GRANDAD'S CARVING PASSION
 Grandad carved a wooden giraffe as he had seen a real one at the Colosseum. Can you find it?

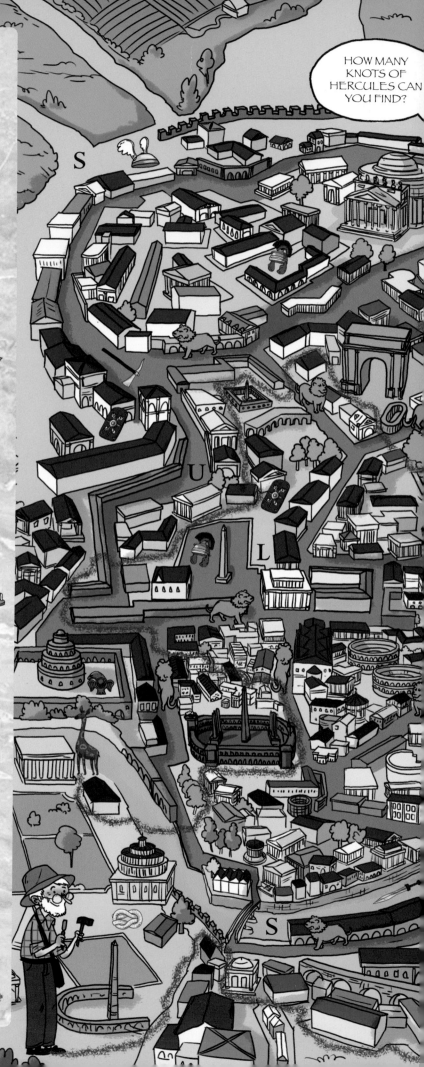

HOW MANY KNOTS OF HERCULES CAN YOU FIND?

ROMAN MOSAICS

Roman houses were so well built that many still exist throughout the Roman Empire. Wealthy Romans liked their buildings to look beautiful as well as being well-made. The floors were often decorated with mosaics, which used tiny pieces of coloured tiles to create patterns and scenes of history and everyday life. Some mosaics were standard designs but wealthy villa owners could afford more personalised designs.

The senator who captured Granny has employed Titus Flavius, a famous forger, to make a copy of a mosaic of Medusa, the snake-headed woman. Compare the original (above) with the forgery (right) and see how many pieces of mosaic he made mistakes with. The senator told him he would pay the forger in coins worth 69 asses. For each mistake in the forgery that you find he will deduct 1 ass.

How many of each of the coins does the senator have to pay?

1 bronze sestertius is worth 4 asses, 1 silver denarius is worth 16 asses, 1 gold aureus is worth 25 asses.

Make sure you get the answer right or the senator will not be pleased!

ROMAN BATHS

Most Roman cities had at least one, but probably many, public buildings for bathing. They were also places to meet up with friends. Bath houses were also built for private villas, town houses and forts.

Zak, Leah and Grandad are at a bath house. Today it has made £60 from swimmers and £8.40 from non-swimmers. Men pay twice as much as women and four times as much as children. Count the number of men, women and children in the pool and the number of non-swimmers (the men on the side wearing togas count as non-swimmers).

Can you work out the price each group pays to swim or watch? Don't forget to include the time-travellers!

Use the maths helper clue box on page 7 if you're stuck.

MEET THE GODS
Apollo was the god of the sun. His symbols were the golden lyre, the snake, laurel and the hyacinth. Can you spot one of each?

COIN
Crocodile coins were minted by the Romans from 28-27 BCE showing a crocodile, the Roman symbol for Egypt, chained to a palm tree, the Roman symbol of victory. Can you find the crocodile coin?

LOST WEAPONS
How many of each of these weapons can you find?

GRANDAD'S CARVING PASSION
Inspired by Apollo, Grandad carved a wooden sun. Can you find it?

Strict father   Funny clown   Smart slave

Moody mother   Braggart soldier   Sad daughter

Happy senator   Slave trader   Merry lawyer

MEET THE GODS
Venus was the goddess of love and beauty. Her symbols were the dove, the swan, the rose, myrtle and the seashell. Can you find the symbols?

COIN
There are some Greco-Roman legends that say ravens were once all white. Because the raven couldn't keep a secret to save its life, Apollo punished the raven by turning its bright white feathers black after it gave away too many secrets. Can you spot the raven coin?

LOST WEAPONS
How many of each of these weapons can you find?

GRANDAD'S CARVING PASSION
In need of milk for his tea, Grandad has carved a wooden cow. Can you find it?

THE CHARIOT RACE

Chariot racing was a popular sport in Roman times. Races were held between small, two-wheeled vehicles drawn by two, four or six horses. The chariots were easily broken when they smashed into each other. The drivers were often entangled in the long reins and dragged to their deaths or seriously injured.

Four chariots set out to race from the starting line. The aim of the race is to end up in the same line-up position you started in, pushing your opponents out of the way as you race around the Circus Maximus. It doesn't matter who crosses the line first. Follow the tracks from the starting blocks and work out which chariot is going to win. Two chariots collided and a wheel came off one of the chariots. Which chariot was it and where did the wheel end up?

MEET THE GODS
Bacchus was the god of wine. He was often shown with a bunch of grapes and a wine cup. He carried a thyrsus, a staff of giant fennel covered with ivy vines and leaves and topped with a pine cone. Can you find it?

COIN
In 284 CE the hippopotamus was brought to Rome by Emperor Philip the Arab to fight gladiators for Rome's 1,000th anniversary. Can you spot the hippo coin?

LOST WEAPONS
How many of each of these weapons can you find?

GRANDAD'S CARVING PASSION
Grandad has carved a wooden horse, hoping it might win the race. Can you spot it?

THE ROMAN EMPERORS' GALLERY

In theory, Roman emperors chose their own heirs. However, many men grabbed power by organising the murder of the current emperor.

The director of The Roman Emperors' Gallery has made several mistakes in the room where the portraits of the Roman emperors hang. Some are not emperors at all! Look at the list of emperors on page 7 to see which are the mistakes below.

Can you work out the average life span of the real emperors? To do this, work out how long each one lived (using the Roman numerals table on page 7), add them together and divide by the number of emperors. Remember not to include the imposters.

So many emperors were murdered, assassinated or committed suicide that the job of emperor seems to result in a shorter life span than average. Is this true? The average life expectancy for people at this point in history was 35 years old.

HOW MANY KNOTS OF HERCULES CAN YOU FIND?

D — TRAJAN — THE KIND-HEARTED SOLDIER
LIII — CXVII CE

MAXIMINUS
CLXXIII — CCXXXVIII CE

JUSTINIAN I — THE LAST 'GREAT' EMPEROR
CDLXXXII — DLXV CE

HADRIAN
LXXVI — CXXXVIII CE

A — TIBERIUS
XLII BCE — XXXVII CE

VITRUVIUS
LXXX — XV BCE

I — CONSTANTINE THE GREAT
CCLXXII — CCCXXXVII CE

ELAGABALUS
CCIII — CCXXII CE

MARCUS TULLIUS CICERO
CVI — XLIII BCE

MEET THE GODS
Medusa had beautiful long hair and was courted by many suitors. One day, Poseidon found Medusa worshipping in the temple of Athena and ravished her. Athena was angry and punished Medusa by turning her beautiful hair into snakes. This gave Medusa the power to turn anyone who looked directly at her into stone. Can you find her eye?

COIN
A powerful bull is shown attacking a wolf. The bull was an ancient symbol of Italy, while the wolf stands for Rome. The Italians were angry because the Romans would not allow them to become Roman citizens even though they were the backbone of the mighty Roman army. So the coin showed what the Italians would like to do to the Romans! Can you find the coin?

LOST WEAPONS
How many of each of these weapons can you find?

GRANDAD'S CARVING PASSION
Grandad has carved a laurel wreath. Can you find it?

NERO
XXXVII – LXVIII CE

CALIGULA
XII – XLI CE

MARCUS AURELIUS
CXXI – CLXXX CE

TITUS
XXXIX – LXXXI CE

HOW MANY EAGLE BROOCHES CAN YOU FIND?

CLAUDIUS
X – LIV CE

FLAVIUS VALENS
CCCXXVIII – CCCLXXVIII CE

GAIUS PLINIUS SECUNDUS
XXIII – LXXIX CE

AUGUSTUS – THE FIRST EMPEROR
LXIII BCE – XIV CE

PUBLIUS VERGILIUS MARO
LXX – XIX BCE

19

HOW MANY KNOTS OF HERCULES CAN YOU FIND?

INSPECTING ROMAN SOLDIERS

The rapid growth and success of the Roman Empire was largely due to the Roman army. It was created to defend the city of Rome but through invasions and wars it helped to conquer a vast empire. Soldiers were paid professionals who joined up for 20 to 25 years.

The army was arranged in legions. Each legion had 5,000 legionaries (soldiers). The legions were divided into centuries of 80 soldiers, led by a centurion.

The soldiers are lined up for inspection. Grandad is examining the soldier on the left so he knows what to look out for. How many faults can you spot in their uniform and weapons by comparing each soldier with the one next to Grandad? Every detail matters! Stand to attention and polish your eyes before you begin!

20

MEET THE GODS
Juno was the queen of all the gods and also the goddess of marriage. She wears a goatskin cloak and has a peacock by her side. She has lost her peacock. Can you find it?

COINS
A camel was a sign of wealth in the ancient world. They were displayed at the Colosseum. Two Roman emperors, Nero and Heliogabalus, had their chariots drawn by rare Bactrian camels. Can you find the camel coin?

LOST WEAPONS
How many of each of these weapons can you find?

GRANDAD'S CARVING PASSION
Grandad has carved a wooden compass to help him find his way. Can you find it?

THE BATTLE OF ZAMA

The Roman army fought battles in many countries to create their empire, which stretched from Britain to Egypt. The Battle of Zama was fought in 202 BCE. The Romans were led by Scipio Africanus. They defeated the Carthaginians of North Africa (an area which is now in modern Tunisia) who were led by Hannibal.

ANIMALS IN BATTLE

The Romans used fierce mastiff type dogs in battles. How many dogs can you spot wearing armour?

The Romans also threw cats at the enemy. How many cats can you find waiting to be thrown, flying through the air or landing on the enemy?

The Romans won the battle after their trumpeters blew their trumpets and frightened the Carthaginian elephant which then charged around, creating chaos. How many trumpeters can you spot?

E

L

HOW MANY
EAGLE
BROOCHES CAN
YOU FIND?

MEET THE GODS
Neptune was the god of the sea. He carries a trident but he has lost it. Can you find it?

Neptune was one of only three Roman gods to whom it was appropriate to offer the sacrifice of bulls. How many bulls can you find?

COIN
As well as using them in battle, the Roman's used dogs for hunting and for guarding the home. Can you find the dog coin?

LOST WEAPONS
How many axes can you find?

GRANDAD'S CARVING PASSION
Wanting to help win the battle, Grandad has carved a wooden elephant. Can you find it?

?

CAESAR MEETS CLEOPATRA

The Romans were famous for building long, straight roads so that the army could march the shortest route between two places. They invaded what we now know as Britain, France, Spain, Morocco, Algeria, Tunisia, Libya and Egypt, as well as most of Eastern Europe, Greece and Turkey. They have left a trail of Roman buildings such as arches, aqueducts, temples, basilicas and amphitheatres. Important trade routes were established throughout northern Africa.

In 48 BCE Julius Caesar took 4,000 men with him on this journey.

Can you follow the roads that lead Caesar from Rome to Alexandria where he met the Egyptian queen Cleopatra? If the land or sea route is blocked, you cannot pass. Make sure the red or blue route you follow is never broken!

Caesar   Cleopatra

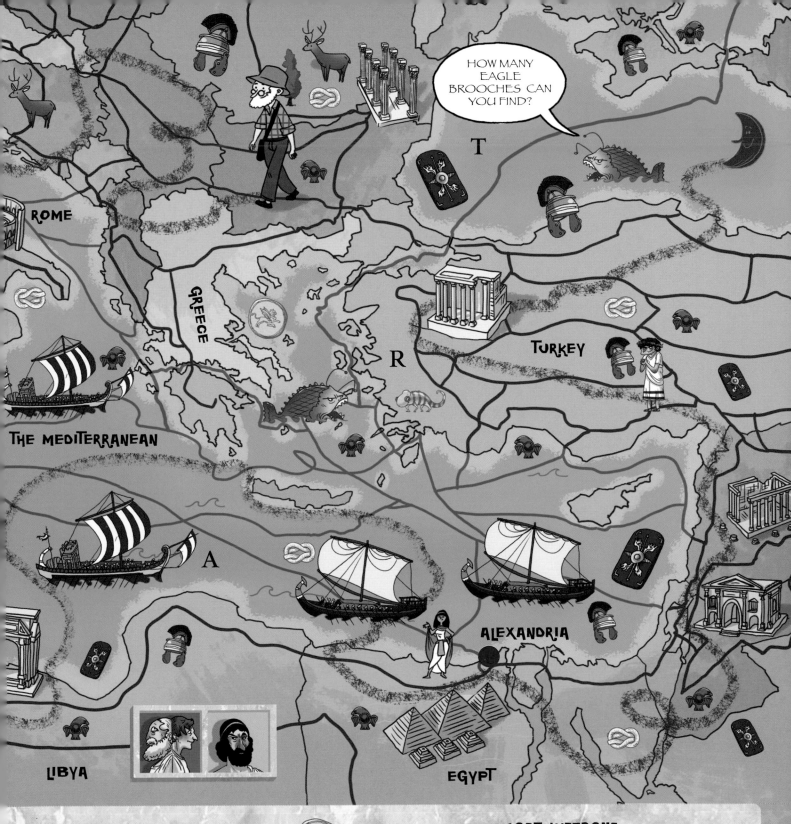

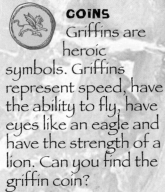

MEET THE GODS
Diana is goddess of the moon and hunting. Her symbols are the cypress tree and the deer. She was worshipped at the Nemoralia Festival of Torches. Can you find the cypress tree? How many deer can you spot?

COINS
Griffins are heroic symbols. Griffins represent speed, have the ability to fly, have eyes like an eagle and have the strength of a lion. Can you find the griffin coin?

LOST WEAPONS
How many of each of these weapons can you find?
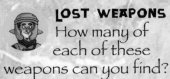

GRANDAD'S CARVING PASSION
Inspired by Diana, Grandad has carved a wooden moon. Can you find it?

THE EMPEROR'S BANQUET

Wealthy Romans sometimes held splendid feasts for their guests. They would be served lots of small dishes such as eggs, olives, figs, snails or oysters. There may also have been treats such as dormouse or lark and plenty of wine. Guests ate with their hands, which were then wiped by slaves.

CATCH THE THIEF

A thief has invaded the emperor's banquet and stolen some of the valuable drinking goblets. When the banquet started, each of the 43 guests had one goblet each. Count the goblets to help Zak and Leah find out how many the thief has stolen.

The thief also stole a crossbow brooch, but was careless. These were worn with the crossbow facing down. In his haste the thief has put it on the wrong way up. Can you catch the thief?

MEET THE GODS

Pluto was the god of death. He ruled the Underworld, which was known as Hades. Black animals were sacrificed to the gods of the Underworld. How many black animals can you spot?

COIN

The sphinx was the symbol of Egypt. It was carved onto this coin in memory of the seal of Augustus, which featured the sphinx. Can you find the coin?

LOST WEAPONS

How many of each of these weapons can you find?

GRANDAD'S CARVING PASSION

Inspired by the feast, Grandad has carved a bunch of wooden grapes. Can you find them?

HOW MANY EAGLE BROOCHES CAN YOU FIND?

LOOK, THERE'S AN ANIMAL STATUE. THAT'S MEDUSA'S WORK. LOOK BACK AND SEE HOW MANY YOU CAN SPOT IN THE BOOK.

ANSWERS

The pictures show you the best routes for the mazes and where to find some of the other objects. If you can't find all the knots and brooches, Grandad's carving and the chameleon, have another go!

The gang of thieves are all wearing a toga like this. Can you find all 10 thieves?

8-9 CITY OF ROME

If you follow the route above you will collect 19 lions.

ANAGRAM: COLOSSEUM

TREASURE: Necklace

LOST WEAPONS: 4 helmets, 6 shields, 5 swords and 1 axe

- There are 4 eagle brooches
- There are 3 knots of Hercules

10-11 ROMAN MOSAICS

There are 20 errors on the mosaic. The senator should pay 49 asses as follows:
1 gold auerus: 25 asses
1 silver denarius: 16 asses
2 bronze sestertii: 4 asses each

ANAGRAM: DOORWAY

TREASURE: Dagger

LOST WEAPONS: 1 helmet, 4 shields, 5 swords and 2 axes

- There are 8 eagle brooches
- There are 5 knots of Hercules

12-13 ROMAN BATHS

If you've not worked out the maths yet, you could look at this clue box on page 7 before you look at the answers!

Swimmers: 20 men, 16 women and 8 children
Non-swimmers: 16 men, 8 women and 4 children
Swimmers prices: The men pay £2, the women pay £1 and children pay 50 pence.
Non-swimmer prices: The men pay 40 pence, the women pay 20 pence and children pay 10 pence.

ANAGRAM: PILLAR

TREASURE: Treasure chest

LOST WEAPONS: 3 helmets, 5 shields, 6 swords and 4 axes

- There are 9 eagle brooches
- There are 7 knots of Hercules

14-15 ROMAN THEATRE

The characters on stage (left to right) are: Strict father, Smart slave, Moody mother, Braggart soldier, Happy Senator, Slave trader

ANAGRAM: WINDOW

TREASURE: Helmet

LOST WEAPONS: 6 helmets, 4 swords and 6 axes

- There are 2 eagle brooches
- There are 6 knots of Hercules

16-17 THE CHARIOT RACE

The chariot with the yellow caped driver is the winner.

The chariot with the blue caped driver lost its wheel in the crowd, lower right.

ANAGRAM: OBELISK

TREASURE: Gold laurel leaves

LOST WEAPONS: 5 helmets, 8 shields, 7 swords and 4 axes

- There are 6 eagle brooches
- There are 6 knots of Hercules

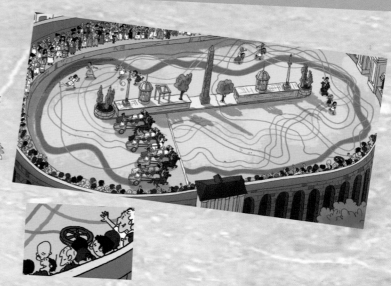

18-19 THE ROMAN EMPERORS' GALLERY

These are the emperors and their dates:

TRAJAN
53–117 CE (64 years)

MAXIMINUS
173–238 CE (65 years)

JUSTINIAN
482–565 CE (83 years)

HADRIAN
76–138 CE (62 years)

TIBERIUS
42 BCE –37 CE (79 years)

ELAGABULUS
203–222 CE (19 years)

CONSTANTINE THE GREAT
272–337 CE (65 years)

NERO
37–68 CE (31 years)

CALIGULA
12–41 CE (29 years)

MARCUS AURELIUS
121–180 CE (59 years)

TITUS
39–81 CE (42 years)

CLAUDIUS
10–54 CE (44 years)

FLAVIUS VALENS
328–378 CE (50 years)

AUGUSTUS – THE FIRST EMPEROR
63 BCE –14 CE (77 years)

ANAGRAM: HADRIAN

TREASURE: Ring

LOST WEAPONS: 1 helmet, 1 shield, 5 swords and 2 axes

- There are 2 eagle brooches
- There are 5 knots of Hercules

Total years: 769

Average life span is 54.92 years so emperors live on average 19.92 years longer than the common man.

20-21 INSPECTING ROMAN SOLDIERS

There are 13 errors on the uniforms.

ANAGRAM: ARCH

TREASURE: Gold armour

LOST WEAPONS: 2 helmets, 5 swords and 3 axes

- There are 4 eagle brooches
- There are 6 knots of Hercules

22-23 THE BATTLE OF ZAMA

There are 7 dogs.
There are 14 cats.
There are 3 trumpeters.
There are 4 bulls.

ANAGRAM: WELL

TREASURE:
Gold bracelet

LOST WEAPONS: 8 axes

- There are 7 eagle brooches
- There are 9 knots of Hercules

24-25 CAESAR MEETS CLEOPATRA

There are 6 deer.
ANAGRAM: THEATRE
TREASURE: Horn
LOST WEAPONS: 9 helmets, 10 shields

- There are 12 eagle brooches
- There are 10 knots of Hercules

26-27 THE EMPEROR'S BANQUET

There are 36 goblets so 7 have been stolen.
There are 3 black animals.

ANAGRAM: STAIRS

TREASURE: Gemstone

LOST WEAPONS: 6 helmets, 8 shields, 5 swords and 6 axes

- There are 6 eagle brooches
- There are 10 knots of Hercules

Thief!

OTHER PUZZLES
GOD'S DOMINOES

26-27

10-11

22-23

16-17

24-25

18-19

14-15

8-9

12-13

20-21

There are 10 more dominoes in the chain. The final domino shows Medusa.

ONE LAST PUZZLE

There are 19 statues that Medusa has made. Can you find them all?

CONGRATULATIONS

If you've solved all the puzzles, the senator will let Granny go!

First published in 2013
by Franklin Watts

Copyright © Franklin Watts 2013

Franklin Watts
338 Euston Road
London NW1 3BH

Franklin Watts Australia
Level 17/207 Kent Street
Sydney, NSW 2000

All rights reserved.

Editor: Sarah Peutrill
Designer: Matt Lilly

Dewey number 937
ISBN (HB): 978 1 4451 1909 0
ISBN (PB): 978 1 4451 1911 3
ISBN (Library ebook): 978 1 4451 2561 9

Printed in China

Franklin Watts is a division of Hachette
Children's Books, an Hachette UK company.
www.hachette.co.uk